This book belongs to:

_____

For Elsie and Gloria, such inspiration,
and thanks to Helen.

This paperback edition first published in 2020 by Andersen Press Ltd.
First published in 2019 by Andersen Press Ltd.,
20 Vauxhall Bridge Road, London, SW1V 2SA

Copyright © Julia Woolf 2019

The right of Julia Woolf to be identified as the author and illustrator
of this work has been asserted by her in accordance with the
Copyright, Designs and Patents Act, 1988.

Printed and bound in China.

1 3 5 7 9 10 8 6 4 2

British Cataloguing in Publication Data Available.

ISBN 978 1 78344 886 9

Julia Woolf

Duck & Penguin
are NOT Friends

Andersen Press

This is Betty and her favourite toy, Duck.

This is Maud and her favourite toy, Penguin.

"Look – they love each other!" says Betty.
"Kiss, kiss, kiss," says Maud.

Betty and Maud are best friends.

Duck and Penguin... are NOT!

Betty and Maud are having a play date.

First they skip to the swings.

weeeee!!!

Betty pushes Maud
all the way up.

Duck pushes Penguin
all the way off.

whaaa!!!

Next, they build sandcastles.
"I love playing in the sandpit," says Maud.

"I bet Duck and Penguin are loving it, too," says Betty.

Inside, it's time for baking.
"Baking is the best," says Maud.
"I love whisking the mixture."
"I love cracking the eggs," says Betty.

Duck and Penguin
love cracking eggs

and whisking the
mixture, too!

While things are baking, there's time for a bit of painting.

"I'm painting Penguin," says Maud.
"I'm painting Duck," says Betty.

splodge!

splodge!

Duck and Penguin are painting each other.

"Oh, now they look a bit... painty," says Maud. "And sandy," laughs Betty. "And eggy!" giggles Maud.

"Never mind," says Betty. "There's nothing better than a good bath."

"Look at them hanging out together," says Maud.
"They really do love each other."

"They're still soggy though," says Maud.
"I know what we need," says Betty.

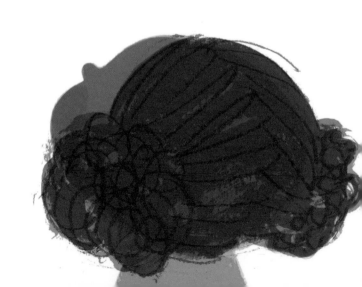

"Not so painty now,"
says Maud.

"Not so sandy
either," says Betty.
"And they're
definitely not
eggy, too."

"Oh they're all fluffed up," says Maud.

"They look so cute,"
says Betty.

"Let's play...

Itty-bitty babies!" says Maud.

"Oh," says Betty,
"we've forgotten
their bottles."
"Let's go and get
them," says Maud.

And off they skip!

But Duck and Penguin really aren't keen
on playing itty-bitty babies.

It's much more fun
going all the way
up on the swing...

weeeee!!!

building sandcastles
in the sandpit...

cracking eggs and whisking mixture...

and a bit of painting...

Quick, Betty and Maud are coming...

"Here are your bottles," says Betty.

"They really do love each other," says Maud.

And perhaps now, they do.

Hee hee Hee   Hee Hee he

Read Duck and Penguin's next adventure...